& Friends. TEAM UP

by Raúl the Third

colors by Elaine Bay

VERSIFY
An Imprint of HarperCollinsPublishers
BOSTON   NEW YORK

3

When he was young, he was THE BEST!

He learned many wrestling styles from the best Lucha Masters.

Doctor Feo!

He made a promise to share his newfound skills.

I will teach the world!

Ricky Ratón taught his students many skills.

Strength training!

Acrobatics!

Discipline!

Patience!

BLA-
LA-
LA-
LA!!

El Toro and his friends each learned
their very own special move!

Lizarda could whip her sticky tongue!

Jack A. López could run circles around anybody!

Croak could bounce like a super ball!

La Oink Oink's over-the-top kicks . . .

. . . never missed their target!

BULLSEYE!

And, last but not least, El Toro
had his . . .

SUPER
CHARGE!

21

All of them were becoming the
best luchadores they could be!

Ricky Ratón takes a swing at Croak and . . .

La Oink Oink uses her sneak
kick, but her teacher is too fast.

But Croak knocks Armor Dillo out of the sky!

El Toro charges!

You can't hit what you can't see.

El Toro and his friends have failed!

43

Celebrating eight World of ¡Vamos! books would not be possible without my incredible team at Versify! This one is for you, Versify Books! —Raúl the Third

This book is dedicated to all who Team Up to help the world, of which we are a part. —Elaine Bay

Versify® is an imprint of HarperCollins Publishers.
Versify is a registered trademark of HarperCollins Publishers LLC.

Copyright © 2022 by Raúl Gonzalez III

Team Up

Library of Congress Cataloging-in-Publication data has been applied for.

ISBN: 978-0-358-39471-6

The illustrations in this book were done in ink on smooth plate Bristol board with Adobe Photoshop for color.
The text type was set in Adobe Garamond LT Std.
Hand lettering by Raúl Gonzalez III
Design by Natalie Fondriest

Manufactured in Italy
RTLO 10 9 8 7 6 5 4 3 2 1
4500844772

First Edition